Eileen Spinelli

# Lizzie Logan
# Is in the Wedding

SIMON & SCHUSTER BOOKS FOR YOUNG READERS

I would like to thank the Shaw family, Larry Pringle, and Phyllis Lane, who taught me about violins, bats, and chopsticks.

To Betty M., Cilla M., Hildegard V.,
Florence K., and Virginia T., who love me
warts and all
—E. S.

SIMON & SCHUSTER BOOKS FOR YOUNG READERS
An imprint of Simon & Schuster Children's Publishing Division
1230 Avenue of the Americas, New York, New York 10020
Copyright © 1997 by Eileen Spinelli

SIMON & SCHUSTER BOOKS FOR YOUNG READERS is a trademark of Simon & Schuster.
The text for this book is set in 14-point Zapf Calligraphic 801.
Printed and bound in Canada
First Edition
10 9 8 7 6 5

Library of Congress Cataloging-in-Publication Data
Spinelli, Eileen.
   Lizzie Logan gets married / Eileen Spinelli. — 1st ed.
              p.          cm.
   Summary: When Lizzie's mother announces that she is remarrying, Heather wonders if her wild and unusual friendship with Lizzie will survive the preparations for the wedding.
   ISBN 0-689-81066-0
   [1. Weddings—Fiction. 2. Friendship—Fiction.] I. Title.
PZ7.S7566Lf 1997
[Fic]—dc20  96-19025

Reprinted by arrangement with Simon & Schuster Books for Young Readers,
an imprint of Simon & Schuster Children's Publishing Division.

Originally published as *Lizzie Logan Gets Married*.

# Contents

1. Wart 1
2. Good News 5
3. Bad Rice 10
4. Rascals 15
5. Bats and Violins 20
6. Fathers 27
7. Almost Halloween 31
8. Surprise 36
9. Chiropterophobia 41
10. When Parents Have a Meeting 46
11. Fruits and Vegetables 51
12. Lizzie's Relatives 59
13. Looking Goofy 63
14. Entertaining Bootsie Woolery 68
15. Cured 76
16. Wedding Customs 79
17. The Big Day 85

# 1

# Wart

On the first day of third grade I woke up with a wart on my thumb.

I ran screaming to my mother.

She inspected it. "Nothing to worry about."

Hah! I thought, getting dressed. Mom isn't the one going off to third grade with a cauliflower growing out of her finger.

I quickly packed my schoolbag.

I rushed through my cornflakes and banana.

Then I ran to the house two doors down. Lizzie would know what to do.

Lizzie Logan was an expert on practically everything. She was also my best friend.

When I showed Lizzie my wart, she didn't say, "Nothing to worry about."

She said, "Christopher crabcakes, Heather! You've got toaditus."

1

"Toaditus?"

"No doubt about it."

"Is it serious?"

Lizzie got a small flashlight. She pried my mouth open and aimed the light. She peered in.

"Lift your tongue up," she said.

I lifted it.

With the tip of her finger she held up my tongue. She peered at it and nodded and went, "Hmm . . . hmm," like a doctor.

"Eh?" I said. It was all I could say with my tongue at attention.

She pulled her finger away. My tongue fell back into place.

"Looks like we got it just in time," she said.

She marched me to the kitchen.

Sam was standing at the stove, flipping an omelet. Sam was Mrs. Logan's boyfriend-soon-to-be-husband and the world's best cook.

His specialty was pancakes, but he only made them on Sundays after church.

"Hey there, Heather."

2

"Hi, Sam."

Lizzie poked her head into the refrigerator. "Sam, where's those mushrooms?"

"In this omelet, old girl."

"I need one fast."

Sam grinned. "Hungry, huh?"

Lizzie grabbed my thumb. She wagged it at Sam. "Heather's got a wart."

He looked. He nodded. "So?"

"So, you get warts from toads."

Sam slipped the omelet onto a plate. "Actually I think they're caused by a virus."

"Exactly," said Lizzie. "Toad virus. That's why we need a toadstool. It's the only cure."

"I don't know," said Sam. "A mushroom isn't quite the same as a toadstool."

Lizzie dug into the omelet and pulled out a mushroom.

"Hey!" yelped Sam.

"Well, I can't la-dee-da around the neighborhood looking for toadstools on the first day of school," Lizzie said. "Anyway mushrooms are just tame toadstools."

She rubbed the mushroom on my wart

for about a minute. "That oughta do the trick."

Mrs. Logan came in with Lizzie's dog, Charley.

"Somebody's going to be late for school," she said.

Sam kissed the tip of Mrs. Logan's nose. "Medical emergency," he told her.

She tried to guess. "Cut? Scrape? Fall?"

Sam pointed to my thumb. "Wart."

Then, grinning, he pointed to Lizzie. "Wartbuster!"

# 2

# Good News

The first thing Kayleen Bitterman did when she saw my wart was raise her hand.

Our teacher, Miss Kelsey, was checking the attendance sheet. At first she didn't notice Kayleen.

So Kayleen began squirming in her seat. Then she started jabbing both arms at the ceiling. Finally she called out, "Miss Kelsey! Miss Kelsey!"

Miss Kelsey looked up from her desk. "Yes, Kayleen?"

"I need my seat changed."

"Why?" Miss Kelsey asked. "Trouble seeing the board?"

"No."

"Well?"

Kayleen made a sour face. She turned my way. "Heather Wade has warts."

5

"Eeeewwwww!" squealed Sue-Ann LeBoon.

"*One* wart," I said.

Miss Kelsey smiled. "Good news, Kayleen: Warts are not contagious."

When Miss Kelsey turned away I stuck my tongue out at Kayleen.

Kayleen hissed, "But they sure are ugly."

At recess Sue-Ann LeBoon called me "warthog."

Erica Chapko bonked me with a Frisbee. It was an accident. She said she was sorry. Still, I was starting to hate this day.

Then I saw Lizzie clapping erasers outside the fifth-grade classroom. Lizzie was two grades ahead of me.

She waved to me.

She tossed the erasers into the air like oranges.

She tried to balance one on her nose. With her eyes to the sky she didn't notice the principal, Mr. Gates, walking behind her. She backed into him. The two of them fell down like dominoes.

The whole playground went bonkers.

"Did you get a detention?" I asked Lizzie after school.

"Why would I get a detention?"

"Because you knocked Mr. Gates on his behind."

Lizzie rolled her eyes. "Well, not on purpose, goosefeet. Besides, the whole thing was his fault. Creeping up on me like that. I could have had a heart attack. I could have dropped dead in my shoes. I could have . . ."

I changed the subject. "Sue-Ann LeBoon called me a 'warthog' today."

Lizzie snorted. "Takes one to know one." She grabbed my thumb and eyeballed the wart. She nodded like a doctor. "The mushroom treatment's working."

"It is?"

"Sure. Look how much it's shrunk since this morning."

I looked. I stared. "How much?"

"Holy macaroni, Heather! Don't you remember? This morning your wart was as big as a golf ball."

"It was?"

"Well, practically."

"Will it ever go away?"

Lizzie draped her arm around me. "It has to. How else can you be a flower girl at Mom and Sam's wedding?"

I felt my mouth drop open. My eyes bulged. I must have looked like a fish. I gasped. "Flower girl?"

Lizzie nodded. "Yep. I decided in math class."

I was stunned. Me—a flower girl. In Lizzie Logan's wedding—well, Sam and Lizzie's mother's wedding.

At first I couldn't think of a thing to say. Then suddenly I thought of a lot of things. The first one out of my mouth was, "Will I get to wear a fancy dress?"

"Yep."

"What color?"

Lizzie whistled through her teeth. "Yeesh! Any darn color you like."

"Wow!"

Then Lizzie gave me a big grin. "Charley's gonna be in the wedding, too."

I couldn't believe my ears. "Your *dog* Charley?"

"Yes, my *dog* Charley," Lizzie snapped. "Who'd you think—Charlie Brown?"

"But dogs can't be in weddings," I told her. Lizzie sniffed. "Says who?"

# 3

# Bad Rice

Mom was in the mudroom scouring rust from an old milk can.

This past summer she and Dad and Uncle Frank had opened an antique shop called The Good Old Days. Since then there was always something in the mudroom to be scoured, scrubbed, painted, or repaired.

Mozart music bounced off the walls.

When I came in, Mom turned the music down. "How was school?"

I took a deep breath. "Well, Kayleen said my wart was ugly. Sue-Ann LeBoon called me 'warthog.' Erica hit me in the head with a Frisbee. And I'm going to be the flower girl at Lizzie's wedding."

Mom pretended to be walloped. "Wow! You had quite a day!" She led me to the kitchen.

We sat down to milk and goldfish crackers. "So," she said. "What shall we talk about first? Warts or weddings?"

I popped a cracker into my mouth. "Weddings!"

"Does Mrs. Logan know about this flower girl business?"

I shrugged. "Lizzie decided in math class."

"Oh. *Lizzie* decided?"

"Yep."

Mom laughed. "Why am I not surprised?"

"I get to wear a fancy dress. Any color I want. And guess what else?"

"What else?"

"Charley's gonna be in the wedding, too."

Mom nearly choked on her milk. "Lizzie's *dog* Charley?"

"Uh-huh. Isn't it exciting?"

"I don't know if exciting is the word."

After dinner the doorbell rang. It was Lizzie. "I came to show you my engagement ring." She poked a sparkly finger under my nose.

Dad looked up from the seven o'clock news. "Who's the lucky fella? Joey Fryola?"

Lizzie screeched. "I'd rather marry his ant farm!"

We went up to my room. Lizzie stood in front of my mirror, flashing her left hand this way and that.

"I can't believe Sam bought you an engagement ring, too," I said.

Lizzie grinned. "Yep. Asked me to be his daughter—all official-like. Even got down on his knees."

"What did you say?"

"I said yes, noodlehead."

I felt happy for Lizzie. Her real father had left when she was a baby. No one knew where he was. Now Lizzie would have Sam.

"So, are you gonna call Sam 'Dad' now?" I asked.

"Nope," she said. "I tried that. When Mom first told me they were getting married."

"Why'd you stop?"

"Bad luck."

"Bad luck?"

Lizzie explained. "I saw this show on public television. It was about ancient China. If the farmers had a good rice crop, they'd walk around saying, 'Bad rice, bad rice.'"

"How come?"

"Because if they said 'good rice' the bad spirits would have been tempted to ruin everything."

I was confused. "What does rice have to do with you and Sam?"

Lizzie plunked herself down on my bed. "If I called Sam 'Dad' now, before the wedding, the bad spirits might ruin everything. Maybe there wouldn't even be a wedding."

I shivered. "You believe in bad spirits?"

"Not really," said Lizzie. "I just want to play it safe."

"What about after the wedding? Will you call Sam 'Dad' then?"

Lizzie shrugged. "Maybe. Maybe I'll whisper it. Around the house. When no one is looking."

"Don't bad spirits look in houses?"

Lizzie hurled a pillow at me. "Not if you keep the curtains closed."

# 4
# Rascals

On Saturday Lizzie gave me another wart treatment.

Sam was out of mushrooms, so Lizzie used an olive. "Looking good," she chirped.

The wart looked the same to me.

We took Charley to Lizzie's backyard to practice for the wedding.

"Go down the aisle," Lizzie ordered.

The aisle was a flagstone path.

I started walking.

Lizzie yelled, "No, no, no!"

"No what?"

"No, you're not walking right."

I sighed. "I'm walking the way I always walk."

Lizzie smacked her knee. "That's the problem. You're not supposed to walk like you always do."

"I'm not?"

"No. 'Cause this is a wedding, noodle-head. Wed. Ding. You're supposed to do a wedding walk."

Lizzie demonstrated. Slowly, stiffly, she put one foot exactly in front of the other.

I had to laugh. "You look like a tightrope walker."

Lizzie gave me a sour ball glare. "Whose wedding is this, yours or mine?"

"Neither," I said. "It's your mom's and Sam's."

"Well, I have news for you," she snapped. "I'm the daughter and that's as close to being the bride as it gets. As far as you're concerned, this is *my* wedding."

"Okay, okay," I said.

I tightrope-walked down the flagstone path. Thirteen times.

Finally Lizzie announced it was Charley's turn. She called him. Charley came galloping into Lizzie's arms, wagging his tail, licking her face.

Lizzie flailed away. "No, no, no!" she shrieked.

16

I could see it was going to take Charley even longer than it had taken me to learn the wedding walk. Just then the three-year-old Woolery twins appeared. They stood outside the fence.

"Hi, Charley," called Betsy Woolery.

"Here, doggie," called Bootsie Woolery.

"Charley's busy," Lizzie grumbled. She had enough to handle without adding a pair of twins. But the Woolery twins didn't leave. They kept calling.

Finally Lizzie groaned and opened the gate. "You can watch if you're quiet."

"I'll be quiet," said Betsy.

"Me, too," said Bootsie.

Then Bootsie noticed Lizzie's hand. "Ooohh—pretty ring!" She crowded closer. "Let me see."

Before Lizzie could say "jumpin' catfish," Bootsie had grabbed the ring right off Lizzie's finger. And before Lizzie could snatch it back, Bootsie popped it into her mouth.

Lizzie howled.

Charley howled.

Mrs. Logan came running. "What's going on here?"

I pointed to Bootsie. "She's eating Lizzie's ring."

Mrs. Logan knelt in front of Bootsie. She cupped her hand under Bootsie's mouth. "Spit it out, Bootsie."

Bootsie clamped her mouth tighter.

"She won't," said Betsy. "She likes shiny stuff."

"I'll get Mrs. Woolery," I said, racing out the gate.

Mrs. Woolery was already heading up the alley. "Those rascals! I told them to stay put."

"They're at Lizzie's," I said. "Bootsie's got Lizzie's ring in her mouth."

No one—not Mrs. Logan or Mrs. Woolery, not me, not Lizzie, not my father—could get Bootsie Woolery to give up the ring.

Finally she just swallowed it.

Sam scooped her up. "Better get her to the emergency room."

The doctor at the hospital said Bootsie

would live. He said the ring would probably take its "natural course."

Mrs. Woolery patted Lizzie's arm. "I'll return the ring when—well, you know."

Lizzie knew. Back home she glowered. "I absolutely refuse to wear a ring that's been pooped out."

Sam ruffled Lizzie's hair. "You won't have to," he told her. "I'll get you another."

"I don't want another ring."

"Then I'll get you a bracelet."

Lizzie scowled. "No, thanks."

"Well, what?" Sam asked. "A necklace? A pin? A silver charm?"

Lizzie flounced over to the sofa. She plopped down. She folded her arms across her chest. "Chopsticks," she said.

# 5

# Bats and Violins

Not only did Sam buy Lizzie a set of chopsticks, he bought a set for me, too. Both sets were bright red. Lizzie made me promise never to use a fork again.

On Monday it took me forty-five minutes to eat a bowl of cornflakes. Lizzie was even slower. She was still chopsticking her way through grapefruit when I stopped by. Mrs. Logan snatched the grapefruit away. She pointed to the door. "School. Now." We left.

"Whatcha gonna be for Halloween?" Lizzie asked.

"Halloween?" I said. "That's over a month away."

Lizzie shrugged. "I like giving myself plenty of time to get my costume together."

"What are you gonna be?"

Lizzie grinned. "A bat."

"Oooo." I shuddered. "I hate bats. They get tangled in your hair."

"They do not, goosefeet."

"Do too," I said.

"Who told you?"

"I don't remember."

"Well, whoever it was had noodles for brains."

"Let's talk about something else," I said.

Lizzie inspected her fingernails. "No. I like talking about bats. Did you know bats are the only mammals that fly?"

I held my ears. Lizzie's voice sounded far away, like it was underwater. Still, I could hear, "In China they believe bats bring good luck. The vampire bat is no bigger than a sparrow. Some bats catch fish with their claws. . . ." Lizzie went on and on like some walking bat encyclopedia.

I was glad when we finally got to school.

After taking attendance, Miss Kelsey brought out her violin. She began to play. Everyone got quiet. I knew the music. It was "Greensleeves," one of Mom's favorites. When Miss Kelsey finished, she announced that she'd be giving violin lessons after school.

On the way home that day, before Lizzie could even think bat, I started talking violin.

I told her how pretty Miss Kelsey played. And how she offered to give lessons. And how five kids had already signed up.

"Did you sign up?" Lizzie asked.

"No."

"Why not?"

"I don't want to learn to play the violin."

"You *have* to," Lizzie said.

"Why?"

"How else can you play a music solo at the wedding?"

"Huh?" I gaped at her. "I thought I was the flower girl."

"You are," she said. "But that doesn't mean you can't be the music, too."

I snorted. "Kids don't play music at weddings."

"Who says?"

I couldn't answer that. Lizzie went on, "All you have to do is play one measly song. I know just the one I want. 'The Hawaiian

Wedding Song.'" She was beaming like a Christmas ball.

"Why don't *you* be the music at the wedding?" I asked.

Lizzie gawked at me. "Are you goofy? Did you ever see a bride play a violin at her own wedding?"

"No, but . . ."

"And do you know why you never saw it?"

"For one thing, because I've never even been to a wedding."

Lizzie waved her arms. "Well, you could have been to a million weddings. A zillion. You'd never see a bride playing the violin. Brides are just too darn busy being brides."

"But you're not the bride," I reminded her.

"Yeesh," whistled Lizzie. "How many times do I have to tell you? I'm the next closest thing to the bride."

I shrugged. "Well, I don't feel like learning the violin."

Lizzie exploded. "*Feel* like? *Feel* like? Did I *feel* like touching your wart? Huh?"

"I don't know."

"Well, I didn't. The only reason I touched it was because we're best pals. Simple as that."

"Okay," I said. "You don't have to touch my wart anymore."

"Hah," she snorted. "Too late. I already did."

When I got home Mom was washing dishes at the sink. I took a deep breath and said it. "Can I take violin lessons?" I expected her to ask me why in the world I wanted to take violin lessons.

She didn't.

Instead, she dropped the dishrag, pulled me to her with soapy fingers, and danced me around the kitchen. Then she said, "I knew there was music in your genes."

First Lizzie.

Now Mom.

Whether I liked it or not, my music career had begun.

That night Mom and Dad and I drove to Music Mart. Mom was positively beaming at the salesman. "We'd like to rent a violin."

Violins come in different sizes. It took a

while, but the salesman finally found one that fit me.

My first lesson was on Friday. Miss Kelsey tuned the violin. Then she showed me how to hold it. Left hand on the neck of the instrument. Bow in the right hand. It sounds easier than it is.

Whenever I slouched, Miss Kelsey tapped me with her pencil. "Posture. Posture."

The clock ticked.

My chin was getting sweaty. My right arm fell asleep.

Finally Miss Kelsey said the magic words. "That's it for today."

I sailed home.

Lizzie was waiting for me on the front porch. She grabbed me by the shoulders. "Play something."

I plopped down on a rocker. "I can't."

"What do you mean you can't? You had your first lesson, didn't you?"

"Yeah," I told her. "But I didn't learn to play a song."

"Well, what *did* you learn?"

I shrugged. "How to hold the violin."

Lizzie howled. "Christopher crabcakes, Heather. Any noodlehead can hold a violin. You don't need lessons for that."

I sniffed. "To hold it correctly you do."

Lizzie began pacing. "The wedding is in three months. We don't have time for all this holding stuff."

"Yeah?" I sneered as I sank into a deep slouch. "Well, tell that to Miss Kelsey."

# 6
# Fathers

The wedding is off.

Here's what happened.

It was seven o'clock at night. Mom and Dad had gone to a movie. Uncle Frank was baby-sitting me. He was back in the mudroom sanding a chair. I was watching a show about humpback whales on public television.

The doorbell rang. It was Lizzie. She looked like she had just lost her best friend. Except that couldn't be true, because I was her best friend.

"What's wrong?" I asked.

She burst into tears. "The wedding's off."

I gasped. "It can't be!"

"Well, it is," she said. "I heard Mom on the phone. Just now. Talking to the church secretary. Canceling everything."

"Everything?"

"Well, the church. In a wedding that's everything, right?"

I led Lizzie to the sofa. We both plopped down. I put my arm around her. "Maybe your mom just changed her mind about a *church* wedding. Maybe they're going to get married in the backyard or something."

Lizzie scoffed. "Oh, right. The backyard. In December. Then everybody can turn into Popsicles."

"Well, in the house then."

"Our house is too small for a wedding," Lizzie sobbed. "I'm telling you, the wedding's off."

I figured Lizzie needed a grown-up. "Let me get Uncle Frank."

She caught my wrist. "No. I don't like people seeing me cry."

"I'm people," I reminded her.

She sniffled. "You're different."

"Well, I have to tell him you're here," I said. "He's going to find out anyway. Unless you want to hide in a closet."

"Just don't tell him why."

I went back to the mudroom.

Uncle Frank looked up from his sanding. "Hi, short stuff."

"You're baby-sitting for two now," I said. "Lizzie's here."

He grinned. "Great. I'll make popcorn."

I shook my head. "I don't think Lizzie's in a popcorn mood."

"Troubles?"

I shrugged.

"Can I help?"

"I think she just wants to talk to me."

Uncle Frank nodded. "Girl stuff, huh?"

"I guess so."

He cut a piece of sandpaper. "Well, holler if you need me."

I patted his shoulder. "Thanks."

I was afraid I wouldn't be much help to Lizzie. I wasn't used to her needing me like this.

We went up to my room. I gave her Pickwick, my favorite teddy bear. Lizzie used to hate teddy bears until she met me. She hugged Pickwick tight.

"It's my fault," she sniffled.

"What is?"

"That Mom and Sam aren't getting married."

"Why is that your fault?"

"Because I'm such a handful. That's what Sam says I am. A handful."

"But I'll bet he smiles when he says it," I said. "Besides, Sam's marrying your mom, not you."

Tears rolled down Lizzie's cheeks onto Pickwick's head. "But I'm part of the deal."

I felt rotten. Lizzie's real father had deserted her. Now Sam. It wasn't fair. Even if she was a handful. I tried to think of something comforting to say. "Maybe *my* dad could be your dad—sort of."

Lizzie's eyes popped. "You mean your dad marry my mom? Isn't that against the law?"

"Not marry your mom, silly," I said. "Just do dad stuff with you sometimes. Like take you to the park. Give you an allowance. Sign your report card. Stuff like that."

Lizzie grabbed a tissue from my nightstand and blew her nose. She wailed aloud, "I want my own father!"

# 7

# Almost Halloween

The wedding is on.

It was never really off.

Lizzie had misunderstood. Her mom did call the church secretary. Did cancel the December date. But not the wedding itself. She just moved the wedding date up. To the second week in November. Lizzie hadn't known that.

Lizzie rushed over to tell me the good news. I'd never seen her so happy. She grinned like a toothpaste commercial. She did little skipping twirls around my bedroom. She even kissed Pickwick.

After that, September flew.

Lizzie and I got dresses for the wedding.

Hers was white satin with gold bows all over it. Mrs. Logan said it was too gaudy. Lizzie said that's exactly why she liked it.

My dress was blue—as soft and billowy

31

as the sky. I chose navy blue shoes with straps to go with it.

Lizzie chose white sneakers and a can of gold spray paint. "I'll have these babies gorgeous in no time," she said.

Sam said Lizzie would fit in perfect at a mummers' parade.

We even shopped for Charley. Lizzie bought him a shiny red bow tie.

At school, I told Miss Kelsey about the change in wedding dates. I told her I had to be able to play "The Hawaiian Wedding Song" by the second Saturday in November.

When she stopped laughing, Miss Kelsey told me I'd be lucky if I could manage "Twinkle Twinkle Little Star."

I practiced the violin faithfully for a half hour every day. Lizzie kept asking for recitals. She said I sounded like a goat stuck under a gate.

I also practiced the wedding walk.

Lizzie stepped up my wart treatments.

❤

Suddenly it was October.

One night Lizzie stopped by to show me

her bat costume. My stomach did a cart-wheel. Fluttery black wings, tiny stitched ears. She—it—hovered over me, grinning.

I backed away.

She whooshed after me.

I shrieked, "I hate bats!"

"No, you don't," she said, flapping her arms wickedly. "You're just scared of them."

"Fine. I'm scared of them."

"Well, you shouldn't be," she said. "They're good. They eat all the bad bugs."

I threw Pickwick at her. "Bats make nests in people's hair."

Lizzie scoffed, "They do not."

"Do too."

"Okay, forget bats," she said, dropping her arms. "What are you going to be for Halloween?"

I told her I didn't know.

"Well, what are you waiting for, goose-feet? Fourth of July?"

"I have time."

Lizzie plunked herself on my bed. She took off her bat ears and wings. "Halloween is gonna be here before you know it. I'm not

33

leaving until you're ready for it."

I sighed. "There's a box of old stuff down in the basement. Maybe I can find a costume in that."

Lizzie jabbed the air with her fist. "Lead the way."

The first thing Lizzie pulled out from the box was a pair of long woolen underwear. Dad used to wear it under his coveralls at his old job, welding ships at the shipyard.

Lizzie dangled it in front of me and cocked her head. "You could be an old hermit. Long underwear. Scruffy beard. Corncob pipe."

I snatched the undies away and tossed them back in the box. "I'm not going to be an old hermit." I held up an old party dress of Mom's. "How about this? I could make a silver crown." I paraded. "Be a princess."

Lizzie pinched her nose. "Now you sound like Kayleen Bitterman."

She rummaged through the box again. "Bingo!" She dragged out a pair of lace curtains. They used to hang in the dining room of the house we lived in before we moved here to Mole Street. They used to be white. Now they were pale yellow.

"It's settled," she announced. "You'll be a bride."

I couldn't see much difference between being a princess and being a bride. I told her so.

She waved me off. "You're not gonna be the pretty, flowery, walk-down-the-aisle kind of bride, noodlehead."

"What other kind is there?" I asked.

Lizzie beamed. "Bride of Frankenstein."

# 8

# Surprise

The wart on my thumb is gone.

Just like that.

I went to sleep Friday night, a girl with a wart. I woke up Saturday morning wartless. Just like Lizzie promised. Her mushroom/olive treatments must have worked.

Still, I wondered: Where did the wart go? I figured it must have fallen off. I decided I'd like to save it. Maybe in some kind of jar with pickle juice. If only I could find the darn thing.

I searched the bed.

I shook the covers.

I crawled under the bed with a flashlight.

No wart.

I started to get nervous.

Maybe I would be walking around my room in bare feet and step on it. Yikes! It might squish between my toes.

Or maybe when I was sleeping some night it would slide down my pillow and into my ear or nostril and I'd have to be rushed, like Bootsie Woolery, to the emergency room.

I raced through my scrambled eggs. I didn't even use chopsticks. I'd sworn to Lizzie that I'd never use a fork again. Nothing, though, about spoons.

Mom said, "Where's the fire?"

"My wart's gone," I told her. "I gotta show Lizzie."

Lizzie was on her front porch chopsticking oatmeal. Little globs fell to the floor. Charley licked them up.

I wagged my thumb. "Look!"

Lizzie eyeballed my thumb. She grinned proudly. She patted her own back. "Good work, girl."

"You should be a doctor when you grow up," I told her.

"Yeah. After I get tired of being a dog trainer and a spider scientist." Then she said she had a surprise for me.

I brightened. "What is it?"

"You won't like it."

"It's something bad?"

"Nope. Good."

"Then I'll like it."

"No, you woooon't," she said in a gooey marshmallow voice.

I clamped my hands on my hips. "Just tell me!"

She did. "Joey Fryola put up a bat house in his backyard."

I squawked.

"It's a blessing in disguise," she went on, draping her arm around me. "Now you'll *have* to learn to get along with bats."

I pushed her arm away. "No, I won't."

"Hey, that's no neighborly way to talk."

"I don't care."

Lizzie shrugged. "I guess that means you don't want to come down with me to see the bat house."

I stomped off her porch. "That's exactly what it means," I called back.

Bats in my very own neighborhood. On my very own street. I couldn't believe it. ·

What's more, I couldn't stand it.

There was only one thing to do.

Mom and Dad were in the kitchen having coffee.

I marched right up to them. I made my announcement: "We have to move."

Mom plunked her cup down. Coffee sloshed over into the saucer. "Hey, I haven't even unpacked all the boxes from *this* move."

"I don't care."

Dad reached up, tweaked my nose. "Fight with Lizzie?"

"No."

"Kayleen being a snit?"

"Kayleen's always a snit," I said. "But that's not why."

Mom pulled me onto her lap. "Then what's the problem?"

I started to cry. "Joey Fryola put up a stupid bat house in his backyard."

"Bat house?" Dad said. "I thought Joey was into ants."

"Ants *and* bats!" I wailed.

Mom smoothed my hair. "Well, we can't move."

I wasn't surprised.

Dad suggested I learn more about bats. Maybe even look at one up close.

Mom suggested I just ignore the whole thing. "After all," she reminded me, "Joey lives at the far end of the street."

I could see I'd have to handle this problem by myself. I slid off Mom's lap. I marched to the basement. I dug all the way to the bottom of the old clothes box. I pulled out Dad's high school football helmet.

# 9

# Chiropterophobia

**M**r. Coleman, the school psychologist, sat on the edge of his desk. He was smiling. Mr. Coleman always smiles. It's like he wants you to think everything's going to be okay.

"So, Heather," he said, "you plan to wear the football helmet in the school building."

I didn't smile. "Yep."

"All day?"

"Yep."

"*Every* day?"

"Yep."

"I see." More smiling.

I twiddled my thumbs. Mr. Coleman took a deep breath. "You know, Heather, it's okay to be afraid of things."

"I know."

"For instance, I'm afraid of heights."

"Yeah." Not that I was interested.

"Absolutely. Get me up on a high bridge and my knees turn to jelly."

"Maybe you should stay off high bridges," I said.

The bell rang for lunch. Mr. Coleman looked at his watch. "Well, Heather—" He stared at me, blinking, smiling. "Let's say you can wear the helmet for a few days."

I nodded. I thought, a few *hundred* days.

He stamped some kind of pink slip and walked me to the door. He patted the top of Dad's helmet. "Everything's going to be okay."

In the cafeteria Kayleen Bitterman pointed at me and snickered.

Sue-Ann LeBoon called me a nut-nick.

Joey Fryola said I was acting like a big baby.

Lizzie hurled bat facts at me like Ping-Pong balls: "Bats make good mothers. . . . A bat knows the sound of her baby's voice. . . . Baby bats are called pups. *PUPS!*" She cooed, "Isn't that cute?"

♥

At my violin lesson on Friday, Miss Kelsey tried to wheedle me out of the helmet. She flung open the closet where she keeps papers and crayons and scissors. "See—no bats." She waved her arms around the classroom. "Not a bat in the place."

I adjusted the chin strap tighter. "Mr. Coleman said I could wear the helmet," I told her. "He said it was okay to be afraid."

"All right." Miss Kelsey sighed. "I guess this is a good time to sing."

"Sing?" I said. "What about my violin lesson?"

"Singing is part of your lesson."

I didn't understand.

Miss Kelsey explained, "You want to learn to play a song, don't you?"

"Yes, but . . ."

"Well, singing the song first will help you learn to play it."

There was no getting out of it. I stood there like a dopey kindergartner and sang "Twinkle Twinkle Little Star." I prayed no one could hear me.

On the way home the clouds got dark.

Fat drops of rain began falling. I wondered how bats felt about rain. Did they want to splash around in it? Or were they huddled in Joey Fryola's house waiting for the storm to pass?

Lizzie was sitting in our living room. She had brought a book to show me. One she'd gotten at a yard sale. It was called *Phobias*.

She skipped through the pages, stopped at the Cs, and pointed. "Here's what you have."

I stared at the word longer than I had at my violin bow: chiropterophobia. Fear of bats.

First toaditus. Now this. "Is there a cure?" I asked.

Lizzie patted my arm. "I'm looking into it." Then she giggled. "At least you don't have clinophobia."

"What's that?"

"Fear of beds."

"Beds? How can anybody be afraid of a bed?"

She shrugged. "People are goofy."

She did some more flipping. She read:

"Vestiphobia. Fear of clothing."

"Holy cow!" I squealed. "What do those people wear?"

"Who knows?" said Lizzie. "Maybe nothing."

"Isn't that against the law?"

"Not in France."

"Suppose you don't want to move to France?"

Lizzie thought for a minute. Then she said, "You could wear a pumpkin. You know, grow one of those humongous state fair prizewinners. Cut out holes for your head and arms and legs."

We wobbled around the living room in pretend pumpkin suits. Bumping into the furniture and each other.

Just then Uncle Frank came in the door. He had his tool chest. Also, a shopping bag full of steel wool.

"Whatcha doing?" I asked.

He tweaked my cheek. "Batproofing the house."

# 10
# When Parents
# Have a Meeting

Life can get really poopy.

It was poopy today.

I forgot my spelling homework.

*And* my math book.

*And* my lunch.

I told Miss Kelsey it was all because of my disease.

"What disease?" she asked.

"Chiropterophobia," I said.

"Huh?"

"Fear of bats."

She stared at me, blinking. "That's no excuse."

I got a zero in spelling for the day.

And I was grounded from recess.

And I had to share Miss Kelsey's lunch: one liverwurst sandwich, two rice cakes, and a box of raisins. My stomach is still squawking.

After school Lizzie informed me that she found the cure for chiropterophobia. "Even checked it out with Mr. Coleman."

I brightened. "What is it?"

"It's the same as the cure for clinophobia, vestiphobia, and all the other phobias."

"Well?"

"It's facing your fear."

I scowled. "What kind of cure is that?"

"The *only* kind, old pal."

"What about pills? What about another mushroom treatment?"

Lizzie shook her head. "None of that stuff works on phobias."

"Not even a doctor's needle?"

"Nope."

At home I took off Dad's helmet. Since Uncle Frank had batproofed the place, I felt safe without it. Also ten pounds lighter.

Mom came into the living room. She sat on the sofa. She patted the seat beside her. "Come here. I have some news."

The last time Mom had some news it

was that she had thrown my purple sun-glasses in the washer with the sheets by mistake.

"Uh-oh," I said, sliding over.

Mom smiled. "Not bad news. Not really."

"Good news?"

"*I* think so."

"Will I think so, too?"

"Could be."

This conversation was going nowhere. "Just tell me," I said.

"Well, we had a meeting."

"Who?"

"All the parents on Mole Street."

"What about?"

"Halloween."

"How come?"

Mom patted my knee. "Because we had concerns. Especially Mrs. Woolery. Bootsie's afraid of the monster masks. And last year Betsy nearly got hit by a car."

"Maybe the Woolery twins should just stay home."

Mom went on, "And then there was Kayleen Bitterman's experience."

"What experience?"

"She got a bad apple."

I gaped at Mom. "With a razor blade in it?"

Mom hesitated. "No—a worm."

"A worm!" I howled. I hadn't been this happy in a week. "So what's the big deal?"

Mom ignored my question. She stroked my ear. "The bottom line is this, sweetie . . ."

Stroking my ear, "sweetie"—this was going to be really bad.

"We've decided not to do trick-or-treating on Mole Street this year."

I shot up from the sofa. "No trick-or-treating? While you're at it, why don't you say no presents at Christmas? No fireworks on the Fourth of July?"

She waved her hand. "Let me get to the good part."

"What?" I growled. "You're gonna leave Groundhog Day alone?"

Mom nodded. "That, too. But the big news is that we're all going to pitch in and have a harvest party."

I stomped off.

I wasn't a bit surprised when Lizzie stormed over like a wild bull. "Harvest party? Harvest party? What do they think we are around here? A bunch of haystacks?"

"No more bride of Frankenstein," I said. "Bootsie Woolery's afraid of monsters."

"Yeah? Well, I'm afraid of Bootsie Woolery. That kid will swallow anything."

"So what can we do?" I asked. "All of Mole Street will be shut down. Everyone will be here." Since no other house was batproofed, Mom had volunteered ours for the party.

Lizzie paced. Scratched her head. Paced some more. Smacked a chair. "Got it!"

"What?"

She gave me her crooked grin. "We refuse to have fun."

"What do you mean?"

"What I mean, jelly brain, is this: We don't eat their stupid party food. We don't join in the games. We don't smile. Period."

I thought about that. "What if somebody tickles me?" I asked.

Lizzie shoved her face into mine. "You bite your tongue."

# 11

# Fruits and Vegetables

**O**nly two kinds of costumes will be allowed at the harvest party: fruit and vegetable.

Lizzie was beside herself. "What's wrong with bats? If it weren't for bats eating up the bugs, there wouldn't even *be* a harvest."

"Can we just not talk about bats," I said.

We were sitting on the floor in Lizzie's room. I was trying to figure out a way to turn an old purple bathrobe into an eggplant.

Lizzie went to the window, flung it open, poked her head out. "Yep, just like I thought."

"Huh?"

"It's still a free country out there. I can talk about bats if I want to. It's called the First Amendment, freedom of speech, in case you forgot."

I stuffed the purple robe into a paper bag. I stood up and marched to the bedroom door. "Fine, you talk bats. I'm going home. It's a free country for me, too."

Lizzie pointed to the floor. "Christopher crabcakes, Heather, sit down. I'll shut up about bats. I'll talk about cabbages and watermelons. How's that?"

"Hey, don't go blaming me," I told her. "This harvest stuff wasn't my idea."

On Halloween afternoon our whole house smelled like a bakery. Doughnut dough sitting on the radiator, rising. Pies in the oven. Cookies cooling.

I remembered my promise: no food, no fun.

But did the no-food rule count *before* the harvest party? Like what if I ate something now?

Mom lifted warm cookies from the pan. "Like to be my taste-tester?"

"No, thank you."

She waved one under my nose. "Chocolate chip."

"Nah—"

"Your all-time number-one favorite."

Did tasting count as eating? Lizzie wasn't there, so I had to ask myself. My self said, No. I took one cookie. I bit into it. I chewed. I felt woozy, it was so good.

Mom stood over me, spatula in hand. "How is it?"

I put on my not-having-any-fun face. I shrugged. "Okay."

She tapped me on the head with the spatula. "Gee, thanks. Don't give me a big head."

That night two turnips rang the doorbell. It was the Woolery twins.

Sue-Ann LeBoon came as an ear of corn.

Joey Fryola wore a pair of his father's green pajamas and a green knit cap.

"What are you?" I asked.

"String bean," he mumbled.

Erica Chapko was a pumpkin.

Kayleen Bitterman was a pink strawberry.

With Dad's help I turned out to be a fairly decent eggplant.

Lizzie arrived last.

She was wrapped in a smelly brown blanket. There was some kind of gray goop in her hair.

Sue-Ann LeBoon squealed, "Eeeewwww!"

Bootsie Woolery took one look and fled to her mother's skirts.

"What the heck are you?" I asked.

Lizzie marched past. She snarled, "A rotten banana."

There was enough food for a whole county of farmers. All the stuff Mom made. A carrot cake from Mrs. Woolery. (She apologized for the poked holes. "I did it!" Betsy beamed.)

There were Sam's candy apples, Mrs. Fryola's *pizzelles*, and Mrs. Bitterman's cherry Jell-O.

The Chapkos and LeBoons brought four pizzas.

I was positively drooling.

Lizzie dragged me into a dark corner. "Remember," she hissed. "No food. No fun."

Sadly, I nodded. I slumped into a chair.

A scarecrow I knew to be Uncle Frank waved a candy apple under my nose.

I waved it away. "No thanks."

"Tummy upset?" he asked.

"Just don't want any."

He offered the apple to Lizzie. Lizzie shook her goopy head.

Uncle Frank shrugged and bit into the apple himself. "Yum."

"Game time!" announced Mrs. Woolery.

"Yippee!" went Betsy.

"I win!" went Bootsie.

Lizzie tapped my shoulder. "I gotta go to the bathroom."

She was gone for a long time. All through pin-the-nose-on-the-pumpkin. When she came back she sat beside me. She burped. Out came a gust of root beer.

I glared at her. "No fair!"

She glared back. "What?"

"You know what. You drank root beer."

"Says who?"

"Says me. I can smell it on your breath."

Lizzie blew into her cupped hands. She took a long sniff. "I don't smell anything."

I stomped off to the kitchen. She followed. "Okay. Okay. I drank root beer," she admitted. "Some dust got caught in my throat. What was I supposed to do. Choke to death?"

"You could have drunk water."

"The root beer was closer."

"You said no food, no fun."

Lizzie smirked. "Exactly. So since when is root beer on the *food* pyramid?"

"You didn't say it was okay to drink at the party."

Lizzie smacked her forehead. "That's because I didn't think I had to. I thought you'd know. People gotta have fluids."

"Right."

"Christopher crabcakes, Heather. Any two-year-old knows that. Do you know what happens to people who don't drink fluids? Huh?"

"What?"

"They dehydrate, that's what. Dehydrate. You know what dehydrate means?"

I had to admit I didn't.

She was in my face. "I'll tell you what it

means. It means you lose all your fluids. Your insides turn to powder, like Kool-Aid before you add water. Your organs shrivel up till they look like peanut shells. Is that what you want? Huh?"

I wasn't sure what human organs looked like, but I knew I didn't want mine looking like peanut shells. I shook my head no.

Lizzie pulled her small flashlight from under her blanket. She aimed the light up my left nostril. "Just what I thought!"

I rolled my eyes down to her while trying to keep my nostril still. "Huh?"

"You're dehydrating fast." She handed me a can of root beer. I drank it down in three gulps. Right away I felt better. I could almost feel my liver pumping up.

We went back to the living room.

Bootsie Woolery was yelling, "I won!"

"No, dear," hushed her mother. "Betsy won."

Bootsie kicked the banister. She yelled louder, "I won."

Mrs. Woolery walked toward Bootsie. "Big girls don't kick," she said.

Bootsie kicked the banister again.

Mrs. Woolery reached out to grab the little turnip.

Bootsie scooted up the stairs, shrieking.

Mrs. Woolery chased after her. I followed.

Bootsie scampered into my bedroom and slammed the door.

I heard a loud crunch. A scream.

I pushed open the door.

Bootsie Woolery was sprawled across a pile of wooden splinters—my violin.

I had been practicing before the party. I forgot to put the violin back in the case.

"Betsy did it!" bawled Bootsie.

My music career was over.

I didn't care what Lizzie thought. I had to break the no-fun rule.

I laughed.

I laughed so hard, my eggplant suit burst apart at the seams.

# 12
# Lizzie's Relatives

The wedding was a week away and Lizzie's house was full of relatives: Sam's parents, Mr. and Mrs. Bright from Arizona; Lizzie's Aunt Iris from California; and Lizzie's Grandma Grace from Maine.

I met them all.

First off, Lizzie's grandmother doesn't look like a grandmother. She has long black hair. Wild hair, really. She wears flowy dresses and sandals.

She doesn't act like a grandmother, either. She says knitting makes her itch, and baking gives her hives. So she writes poems instead. She raises herbs. She already has her date for New Year's Eve. Also, she doesn't eat anything with eyes. That's her way of saying she's a vegetarian.

Aunt Iris is tall and thin. She wears glasses and smells like a peppermint. She's cheery, especially when she's talking medical problems. "Had the worst case of measles the doctor ever saw—ha ha ha!"

When Lizzie told Iris why I was wearing Dad's football helmet, she got positively jolly. "Chiropterophobia! Wow!"

Like Sam, the Brights were kitchen whizzes. At Lizzie's, eggs cracked, butter sizzled, flour flew. Muffins, waffles, enchiladas, homemade pizza.

I happened to be there Monday night at suppertime. Mr. Bright handed Grandma Grace a piece of garlic bread. Grandma Grace yelped and jumped up from the table.

"What's the matter, Mom?" said Mrs. Logan.

Grandma Grace pointed to a sliver of stuffed green olive on her bread.

It did look like an eye.

Mr. Bright chuckled. "I'm a kidder, I am."

❤

Lizzie said she loved having the relatives, except when she had to use the bathroom.

"There's always a line," she grouched. "Sam's dad takes the *National Geographic* in with him. Grandma Grace meditates in the tub. Aunt Iris rearranges our medicine cabinet. I'm gonna get kidney problems."

At least twice a day Lizzie had to run over to use our bathroom.

I could see this wedding business wasn't easy.

While Sam and the Brights baked wedding cookies and hams, everyone else cleaned. Drapes soaked in Lizzie's laundry tubs. Rugs lay under a lather of shampoo. After school Lizzie and I were handed a bottle of Windex and some old undershirts and were pointed in the direction of the windows.

Not even Charley escaped. Grandma Grace decided he needed a bath, too. She set Lizzie's old pool in the basement, filled it with soapy water, and plopped Charley into it. Charley had other ideas. He leaped out of the pool and ran. It took Grandma Grace half an hour to catch him. "There's nothing slipperier than a wet dog," she sighed.

Late Tuesday afternoon I helped Lizzie spray paint her sneakers. Gold.

When the paint dried, Lizzie glued four bows and six stars on each shoe.

Then she eyeballed Dad's helmet. "That's next."

"Huh?"

"Look, goosefeet, it's bad enough you're wearing a football helmet to the wedding. But a green and purple one? Christopher crabcakes, at least it should match your dress."

She decided we'd go buy some blue paint after school on Wednesday.

Back home, I took Dad's helmet off. It seemed to be getting heavier, hotter. I was getting tired of wearing it.

I wished Uncle Frank could batproof Lizzie's house, too. And school. Maybe even the whole entire neighborhood.

# 13

# Looking Goofy

**W**hat's the paint for?" asked the hardware store clerk.

Lizzie pointed to the helmet on my head.

The clerk smiled. "Changing teams, eh?"

"No," said Lizzie. "Chiropterophobia."

"Huh?"

"Medical problem," Lizzie whispered.

The clerk gave me a sad look. And a discount on the paint.

"You have to take it off." We were in Lizzie's room. She was tugging at the chin strap on Dad's helmet.

I pushed her hands away. "No!"

Lizzie gazed at the ceiling. She sighed. "How the heck am I supposed to paint the stupid helmet when it's on your head?"

"I don't know."

"Well, I don't either," she snapped. "It has to come off."

"No." I backed away. "I'm scared."

Lizzie's tone turned as soft as pudding. "There's nothing to be scared of, old pal. You think I'd let anything hurt you? Huh? My very best friend. Huh? Do you?"

I shrugged.

"Well, I wouldn't. I'd smack a black widow if it crawled up your arm. I'd bop a pig on the snout if it tried to eat you. I'd . . ."

"Okay. Okay."

"Okay?" she cooed. "Okay, you mean you'll take the helmet off?"

"No," I told her. "But okay, I believe you wouldn't let anything hurt me."

"Jumping catfish, Heather. Give me the darn helmet."

I looked around Lizzie's room. "Maybe if I had something else to wear. You know— while you're painting the helmet."

Lizzie poked around her room. Under the bed. Nothing. Then she snapped her fingers. "Wait here."

She ran downstairs. When she came back

she had a bag full of stuff. Soup pots, salad bowls, colanders. She beamed. "Take your pick."

I picked a soup pot.

The instant Lizzie lifted the helmet off, I jammed the soup pot on. I could hardly see.

Lizzie got the giggles. "Now you really look goofy. Look in the mirror."

I looked. She was right. I did look goofy. I got the giggles, too. I giggled so hard and so long, I got the hiccups.

Naturally Lizzie knew the cure. "Drink a glass of water down fast while holding your nose."

It worked.

Soon we settled down. Lizzie painted. In minutes Dad's old football helmet was blue.

Lizzie eyed it from all angles. "Needs more," she said. She pulled a box from her closet. From the box she took two peace doves she had made from paper cups in third grade. She glued them to the front of the helmet. Next she glued on two pink plastic roses. Finally four white pom-poms left over from the Fourth of July.

"Wow!" said Lizzie. "You're gonna turn more heads than the bride."

"Don't you think it's too fancy?" I asked.

Lizzie waved me off. "Too fancy? Heather, nothing's ever too fancy for a wedding."

It was getting late. "I have to go home," I said.

Lizzie nodded. "I'll get a box for the helmet."

"What box?" I said. "I don't need a box. I'll just wear it."

Lizzie squealed. "You can't wear it. You can't wear it till the day of the wedding."

"Why not?"

"Because it's bad luck to let anyone see you in your wedding stuff."

"I thought that was just the bride."

"Well, you thought wrong."

"What am I gonna wear till Saturday?"

Lizzie shrugged. "Sam's soup pot, I guess."

I squawked. "I can't walk around in public with a soup pot on my head!"

"No? But you can spoil my wedding, right?"

I didn't want to spoil the wedding. I sighed. "Oh, all right."

Lizzie patted my arm. "Good girl." Then she set the wedding helmet in a cardboard box and covered it with a pillowcase.

I carried it out into the hall. Lizzie checked the living room for relatives. None there. "Coast clear," she whispered to me.

I tiptoed down the stairs. The soup pot wobbled on my head. "This is stupid," I hissed, on my way out the door.

Lizzie hissed back, "So's being scared of bats."

# 14
# Entertaining Bootsie Woolery

The next morning I got ready for school. Jeans. Shirt. Sneakers. Jacket. Soup pot.

Mom planted herself at the door. "Take it off."

"What?" I asked.

She folded her arms. "As if you didn't know."

"Lizzie says I can't wear Dad's helmet. Not till the wedding. If I do I'll bring bad luck."

"Then the wedding's already doomed," Mom said. "You've been wearing Dad's helmet for weeks."

"Yeah, but this is the last couple days. This is when it really counts. Plus, it's decorated."

Dad walked into the living room. "My helmet? What about it?" He kept staring at my head, like he wasn't sure who I was.

"Your daughter decorated it."

He looked at Mom, back at me. His mouth opened but nothing came out.

"Show us," Mom said.

I shook my head. "Nobody can see it. Not till Saturday."

Mom slumped to the sofa. She threw her arms in the air. "I give up."

Dad sat beside her. He brushed a wisp of her hair back. "Don't worry, honey. I'll call Mr. Coleman. He'll know what to do."

Mom nodded.

Mr. Coleman didn't know what to do. So he told Dad to keep me home the next two days. Meanwhile, he'd consult with another psychologist.

Mom returned the soup pot to Sam.

Dad said I could write my spelling words three times each.

After school Lizzie stopped by. "Miss Kelsey sent these home," she said, handing me a stack of worksheets.

I took the papers and set them on the table.

"You look grumpy," Lizzie said.

"I am grumpy," I told her. "I can't even go to school till after the wedding."

Lizzie gawked at me. "Two days off school—*excused*—and you're complaining. What are you? Goofy?" She left.

That night Mrs. Woolery called. She asked Mom if Bootsie could come over for an hour.

The Fryolas had agreed to take Betsy. If we could take Bootsie, then Mrs. Woolery might be able to finish sewing the twins' dresses in time for the wedding.

Mom said sure. When she got off the phone she turned to me. "Heather, you'll have to entertain Bootsie Woolery. I've got laundry to do."

Immediately I hid my mood ring in my sock drawer.

At seven o'clock Bootsie and her mom showed up.

"Bootsie brought a book along," said Mrs. Woolery.

Bootsie patted the book under her arm. She grinned. "It's from Mrs. Fryola."

Mom smiled. "That's nice, Bootsie. Heather will read it to you."

Mrs. Woolery kissed Bootsie good-bye, then she left for some peaceful sewing.

Mom went to the basement to work on the wash.

I took Bootsie up to my room.

Bootsie thrust her book in my face. "Read."

I gaped at the cover. I yelped. "This book is about bats!"

"*Stellaluna*," she managed to say.

I dropped *Stellaluna* on my bed. I pulled a book about elephants from my book rack. "Here's *Baby Elephant*," I said. "I'll read *Baby Elephant*."

Bootsie pouted. She stomped her foot. She pointed to *Stellaluna*. "That book!"

"No, Bootsie," I said.

Bootsie howled. "*Stellaluna!*"

"*Baby Elephant*."

"*STELLALUNA!!!!*"

Bootsie's face was as red as a cherry pepper. Fat tears rolled down her cheeks.

I groaned. I decided I was safe with a

book-bat. "All right. Calm down. I'll read *Stellaluna*."

We sat on the bed together, Bootsie with her knees up, tears gone. I opened the book. I began to read, "'In a warm and sultry forest far, far away, there once lived a mother fruit bat and her new baby.'"

Bootsie pointed to the picture. "Stellaluna's mommy."

"Yes," I said.

"She's pretty," said Bootsie.

"For a bat," I said.

When I finished the book, I was surprised to discover a tear in my own eye. I had to admit that Stellaluna was a cute little thing. And I was glad when her mother found her. But then, Stellaluna was only a storybook bat.

"Let's play Candyland," Bootsie said next.

I got out my old game. "You set it up," I told her. "I'm going to the bathroom."

When I left, she was busy setting up the game.

When I came back, she was nowhere in sight. I looked in the closet and under the bed—and then I heard the front door slam. By the time I got down to the front step, she was gone.

I screamed into the night, "Bootsie!" I ran to the sidewalk. My heart was thundering. "Boot-seeee!"

"Stellaluna! Stellaluna!"

Her voice came from up the street. "Thank you," I whispered and ran.

I followed her voice—"Stellaluna!"—a car honked, icy breath flew in my face—"Stellaluna!"—and suddenly there she was, standing still, pointing up.

I fell to my knees and grabbed her. I don't think I ever hugged anybody so hard. Sobs of relief burst out of me. I squeezed harder. "Bootsie."

Bootsie wriggled one arm free and jabbed it upward. "Stellaluna!"

And just then, that moment, I realized where I was—in Joey Fryola's backyard. And Bootsie's finger pointed to a swirling spiral of batwings overhead.

I shrieked and cringed and covered my head with my arms—and waited for the attack. And waited. But all I felt was Bootsie tugging on my sleeve and pleading, "Look! Look!"

Finally I did, I looked. Wings fluttered like black butterflies in and out of the light from a nearby back porch. Watching the bats swirl, I thought of a merry-go-round— a dark, silent, night-sky carousel. I wondered if one of them was Stellaluna, a pup, as Lizzie would say, clinging to its mother, scared of owls.

A gust of wind blew. I shivered. "Time to go back," I told Bootsie, lifting her up.

She wrapped her chubby arms around my neck. She patted my cheek. "Don't be scared," she said.

I had to laugh. Imagine—a three-year-old telling *me* not to be scared.

"I'm not so scared," I said.

Bootsie waved. "'Night, Stellaluna. Sleep tight."

"Don't let the bedbugs bite," I added.

I carried Bootsie up Mole Street. By the time we reached my house, she was sound asleep.

Mom was waiting, scowling, on the porch. She took Bootsie from my arms. "Where the heck were you? I was ready to call Daddy and Uncle Frank."

"Bootsie wanted to say good night to Stellaluna," I told her.

"Stella *who*?"

"Stella*luna*. A baby bat. From her book. She thinks it lives in Joey Fryola's bat house."

Mom's eyes popped like a bullfrog's. "*You* were down at the Fryolas'? Saying good night to a *bat*?"

I shrugged. "Sort of."

Mom threw her hands in the air. "I give up."

# 15
# Cured

**W**hat do you mean Bootsie Woolery cured you?" Lizzie asked.

"It's hard to explain," I told her.

She shot me a sour ball glare. Lizzie was used to being the medical expert on Mole Street. Now she was upstaged by a three-year-old.

All the way to school Lizzie didn't say a word.

When I walked into the classroom without my helmet, Kayleen Bitterman nearly fell off her chair. Erica Chapko applauded. Miss Kelsey sent me to Mr. Coleman's office.

I told Mr. Coleman about Bootsie Woolery and Stellaluna and the spiral of bats in the night.

He scratched his head. "How old did

you say this Bootsie Woolery is?"

"Three."

He sighed. "I see."

"Maybe she'll be a psychologist when she grows up," I said cheerfully. "Just like you."

"Right." Mr. Coleman led me to the door. He patted my shoulder. "Come back anytime."

After school I met Lizzie on the steps.

"What do you mean you're not wearing the helmet in the wedding?" she said, finally responding to something I said that morning.

"I don't need it."

"But I painted it," she grumbled. "I decorated it. I even used my peace doves, for cryin' out loud."

"I know. And you made it look real nice."

"Nice? Nice?" She was screeching. "Try spectacular! And all for what? For nothing?"

"Sorry," I said. I couldn't look her in the eye. We walked in silence for a while. She calmed down. She put her arm around me. She smiled. "Look, old pal, just because you're cured doesn't mean you can't wear the helmet."

I stared at her. "Huh?"

"Just think of the helmet as a hat."

"Hat?" I said. "That darn thing weighs a ton. It practically covers my eyes. It's got a chin strap. And I'm sick of it."

Lizzie's arm went away. "Fine. Don't wear it."

"I won't."

"Fine."

"Fine."

Lizzie went into a pout. We walked three blocks without speaking. Then she snapped her fingers. She turned to me all smiles. "Okay," she said. "*I'll* wear the helmet!"

# 16
# Wedding Customs

Someone had shaken me awake. The room was dark. The clock on my nightstand flashed 5:15 A.M. I sat up. I blinked a few times. The "someone" came into focus. It was Lizzie, in her frog pajamas and bunny slippers.

"Who let you in?" I whispered.

Lizzie whispered back, "Your dad."

"Dad's awake?"

"Not exactly. But he did answer the door."

I turned on the light. Lizzie looked upset. "What's wrong?" I said.

She crumpled onto the bed. "Sam's gone."

"What?"

"Sam's gone. I woke up with a stomach full of butterflies. I figured I'd ask Sam to fix me some peppermint tea. I couldn't find him."

"Did you look in his bed?"

Lizzie sniffled. "I looked in everybody's bed."

"Sofa?"

"Aunt Iris was on the sofa."

"Did you ask anybody about Sam?"

She rolled her eyes. "Jumping catfish! It's not even six A.M. You think I'm gonna wake up the entire house?"

I shrugged. "You woke *me* up."

"You're different."

It wasn't like Lizzie to be so concerned about bothering people. I told her so.

She gave me a crooked smile. "Okay—I was afraid to ask."

Lizzie afraid? That was a new one. "Afraid of what?"

"Of what I'd find out."

I shook my head. "You'd find out where Sam is, for gosh sakes. Isn't that what you want to know?"

She folded her arms. "I don't know." She shivered as if she were cold. "What if he's just . . . gone?"

"What do you mean?"

Lizzie's eyes filled up with tears. "Gone. G-O-N-E. Like my real father."

I put my arm around her. "Lizzie, Sam wouldn't do that."

Just then Mom appeared, barefoot and wrapped in her pink bathrobe. She pointed to the clock.

Lizzie gave Mom a tiny wave. "Morning, Mrs. Wade."

Mom waved back. She slumped into the rocker, her mouth fell open. Out crawled a single word: "What?"

Mom's always been a one-word person till she's had her coffee.

"Sam's gone," I said.

Mom nodded. "Yes."

Lizzie and I screeched together, "You know?"

"Yes."

My mom's eyes were shut. I shook her. "Well, where is he? Lizzie's worried sick."

Mom's mouth opened a crack. "Frank's."

"*Uncle* Frank's?"

She nodded, her chin bouncing on her chest.

Lizzie smacked herself on the head. "My brains are turning into jelly."

"Huh?" I said.

Lizzie went on. "Of course Sam's not there. He *couldn't* sleep at our house last night."

"Why not?" I asked.

Mom staggered out the door. She croaked over her shoulder, "Custom."

Lizzie nodded. "The groom isn't allowed to see the bride before the wedding. And I just plain forgot."

Suddenly I was tired again. "So everything's okay?"

Lizzie stood up. She beamed. "*Super* okay!"

"Good." I flopped back onto my pillow. "Good night."

I heard Lizzie humming as she bounced down the stairs.

An hour later she was shaking me again. I groaned. "Now what?"

Lizzie twirled around twice. "How do I look?"

I sat up. I rubbed the sleep from my eyes.

I checked her out: fancy helmet, white dress with gold bows, gold sneakers, ratty purple socks. The ones I remembered Charley chewing on weeks ago.

"What's with the socks?" I said.

She grinned. "Great, huh?"

I pinched my nose. "Gross."

"That's because they're old."

"So why wear old socks on your mom's wedding day?"

"Because they *are* old, noodlehead."

I didn't understand.

Lizzie explained. "It's another wedding custom. Something old. Something new. Something borrowed. Something blue."

"Who made up all these goofy customs?" I asked.

She shrugged. "Whoever invented weddings." She pointed to her dress—"New." Then to Dad's helmet—"Blue *and* borrowed. He gets it back tomorrow."

I eyeballed the helmet's paper cup peace doves, pink roses, white pom-poms, gold bows. "I don't think Dad'll take it back," I told her.

# 17
# The Big Day

Finally it was really time for me to get up.

The sun spilled across my room. The smell of coffee filled the house. My flower girl dress hung from the closet door like a blue cloud. This would be my very first wedding. I had a few butterflies of my own.

Dad had gone out for doughnuts. He held one under my nose. "Chocolate glazed," he said.

I shook my head. "No thanks."

Mom was on her second cup of coffee. "Nervous, sweetie?"

I smiled weakly. "Sort of."

She tweaked my cheek. "You'll do fine."

I took three sips of orange juice. Then I went up to get ready. Mom did my hair. She fastened her pearl comb into one side. Then she stood back. "Pretty as a picture."

"Yeah?" I turned to the mirror. I couldn't

say it, but she was right. "Can I go to Lizzie's now?"

I found Lizzie in her room. She had a peanut butter sandwich in one hand and a blueberry muffin in the other. "Fortifying myself for the big day." She grinned. Then she made me turn around. "Wow!" she said. "You look almost as pretty as me."

I could feel the excitement in Lizzie's house. Charley barked and chased and nudged my arm for a scratch. Sam's mother called up to see if I wanted a muffin. Lizzie's grandmother poked her head in the doorway. "I need some help with my zipper," she said.

Since Lizzie's hands were occupied, I zipped Grandma Grace into her flowy, polka-dot dress—careful not to catch her wild black hair.

Aunt Iris borrowed Lizzie's small flashlight. She opened her mouth wide. She aimed the light down her throat. "I'm definitely catching something," she said cheerfully.

Lizzie swallowed her last bite of food.

She brushed crumbs from her dress. Then she grabbed my hand and pulled me down the hall to her mother's room. She opened the door and flung out her arm. "Ta-da! My mother, the bride."

I gasped. Sitting on the bed, looking like a princess, was Mrs. Logan. She was wearing a pink gown, all swishy and soft. On her head was a crown of white and pink roses. I had never seen anyone so beautiful in all my life.

We rode to the church in a line of four cars. Our car was second. Lizzie, Charley, and I sat in the backseat. Halfway there Lizzie said, "I think I'm going to throw up."

Dad cried out, "No! Loosen the chin strap. Open the windows."

Mom kept glancing over her shoulder. "Deep breaths, Lizzie. Big, deep breaths."

Charley barked.

I wagged my finger at Lizzie. "You shouldn't have eaten so much breakfast."

When we got to the church, Joey Fryola was waiting on the steps. He had agreed to stand outside with Charley. I had been right. Dogs can't be in weddings. At least not church weddings.

Lizzie gave Joey and Charley the titles of "Official Greeters."

Charley, bow tie in place, greeted Joey with a growl.

Lizzie growled at Charley, "Be friendly."

The wedding party—Mrs. Logan the bride, Aunt Iris the maid of honor, Lizzie the daughter and me the flower girl—were led into a side room.

Everyone else went into the church.

A table in the side room held all the flowers. There was Mrs. Logan's rose bouquet, a smaller rose bouquet for Aunt Iris, the two baskets of rose petals—one for me, one for Lizzie.

Aunt Iris began to sneeze. The minister appeared. He said, "Bless you," to Aunt Iris. He patted Mrs. Logan's hand and my head. Then he spotted Lizzie's helmet. Suddenly he looked like a fish, all eyes and open mouth.

Lizzie beamed. "Bet you never saw anything like this before?"

He shook his head.

"Designed it myself," said Lizzie proudly.

The minister nodded. "I see. Very nice." He looked at Mrs. Logan. She smiled. He smiled. He looked back at Lizzie. He reached out and rapped the helmet once with his knuckle. "Very good . . . terrific . . ." He clapped his hands. "Okay, time to take it off. Time to walk down the aisle."

"It stays on," said Lizzie pleasantly. "This is how I go down the aisle."

The minister went fish-faced again. He looked at Mrs. Logan, who was still smiling. He seemed to stare at that smile of hers for an hour. Maybe that's where he found the answer, because suddenly he gave a snappy nod and said, "Okay, let's go."

Lizzie tightened the chin strap and grabbed a basket of petals. "Let's get this show on the road."

The church aisle seemed very long, like the yellow brick road in *The Wizard of Oz*.

At the end stood Sam in a navy blue suit. With him were Uncle Frank, who was best man, and the minister. All three were looking up the aisle and smiling at us.

The organist began to play the "Wedding March."

Lizzie squeezed my hand. She was sweating. A minute before, the pews had been filled with backs of heads. Now they were all faces, every one of them. Lizzie started walking. Her golden sneakers sparkled with each step. The helmet bobbed loosely on her head.

I followed, slowly, stiffly. One foot exactly in front of the other. Just like Lizzie had taught me.

We tossed rose petals.

Someone was giggling.

Was I walking wrong? Was my hair sticking up? Was my underwear showing?

I glanced back. It was the Woolery twins. They were in the aisle, stuffing rose petals into their pockets.

Mrs. Fryola and Mrs. Woolery scooped the twins away to the back of the church.

Finally our wedding party reached the altar.

Lizzie and I stepped to one side.

Sam took Mrs. Logan's hand in his. They stood in front of the minister, who said a long prayer.

Next the minister asked Sam and Mrs. Logan a lot of questions. Stuff like, "Do you promise to love each other," et cetera.

I guess he wanted to be sure they didn't goof up, because he gave them the answers.

Then the minister called Lizzie forward.

Lizzie squeezed between her mom and Sam. Sam draped his arm around her.

The minister talked some more. This time about families. He said another prayer. Finally he said, "I now pronounce the three of you husband, wife, and family."

Sam kissed Mrs. Logan. For about an hour. Then he pulled off Lizzie's helmet and lifted her up and hugged and kissed her. Then all three of them were hugging and kissing.

Finally they turned around to face the audience. They were holding hands. No helmet could hide their smiles.

Everybody stood up and cheered and

clapped. There were even a couple of two-fingered whistles.

All three of them were crying—Lizzie's mom, Lizzie, and Sam.

Lizzie pulled a wad of toilet paper from the sleeve of her white satin dress and blew her nose.

Then she looked at me. She waved. And suddenly my own eyes were blurry. I couldn't get over it. Lizzie Logan. My best friend. Since the day I moved to her neighborhood she had always seemed so big and strong and in control. But now she was just one happy little girl, scrunched between her mother and a father all her own.